THE LEGEND OF FREEDOM HILL

LINDA JACOBS ALTMAN
ILLUSTRATED BY
CORNELIUS VAN WRIGHT & YING-HWA HU

LEE & LOW BOOKS INC. • NEW YORK

LEE & LOW BOOKS Inc., 95 Madison Avenue, New York, NY 10016
www.leeandlow.com

Printed in Hong Kong

Book Design by Tania Garcia
Book Production by The Kids at Our House

The text is set in New Baskerville.
The illustrations are rendered in watercolor.

10 9 8 7 6 5 4 3 2 1
First Edition

Library of Congress Cataloging-in-Publication Data
Altman, Linda Jacobs.
The legend of Freedom Hill / by Linda Jacobs Altman ; illustrated by Cornelius
Van Wright and Ying-Hwa Hu.— 1st ed.
            p. cm.
Summary: During the California Gold Rush Rosabel, an African American, and
Sophie, a Jew, team up and search for gold to buy Rosabel's mother her freedom
from a slave catcher.
ISBN 1-58430-003-5
[1. Gold mines and mining—Fiction. 2. Fugitive slaves—Fiction. 3. Slavery—
Fiction. 4. Afro-Americans—Fiction. 5. Jews—United States—Fiction. 6.
California—Fiction.] I. Van Wright, Cornelius, ill. II. Hu, Ying-Hwa, ill. III. Title.
PZ7.A46393 Lg 2000
[Fic]—dc21   99-047893

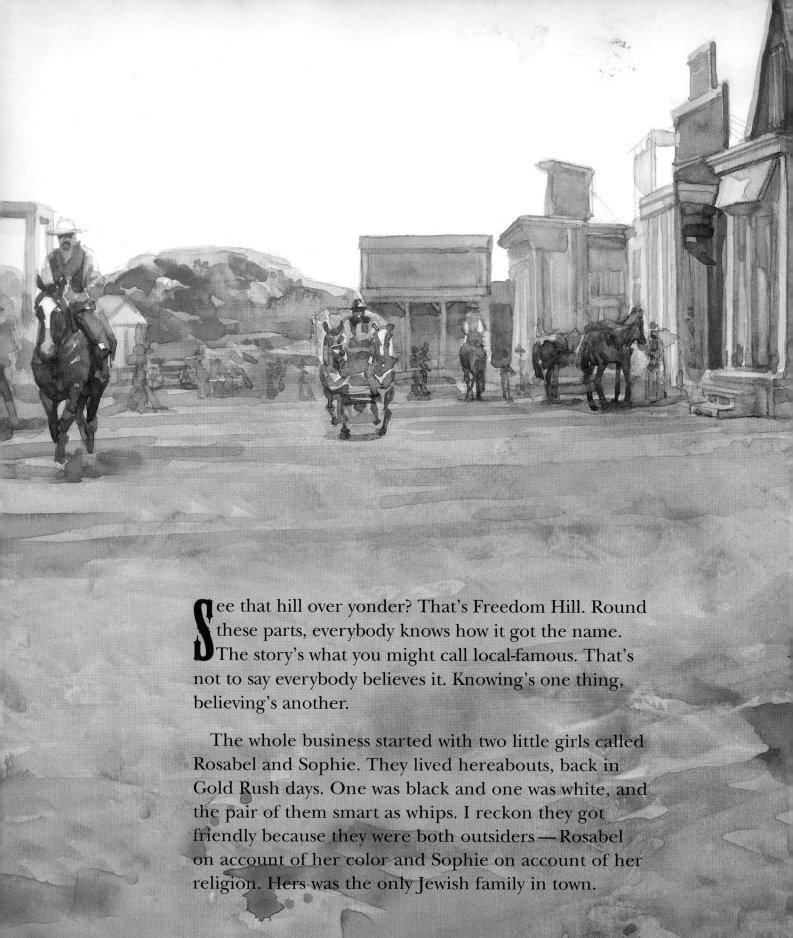

See that hill over yonder? That's Freedom Hill. Round these parts, everybody knows how it got the name. The story's what you might call local-famous. That's not to say everybody believes it. Knowing's one thing, believing's another.

The whole business started with two little girls called Rosabel and Sophie. They lived hereabouts, back in Gold Rush days. One was black and one was white, and the pair of them smart as whips. I reckon they got friendly because they were both outsiders — Rosabel on account of her color and Sophie on account of her religion. Hers was the only Jewish family in town.

Now Rosabel had freedom papers, but her mama didn't. Miz Violet was a runaway slave. Seems some abolitionists from up north raised enough money to buy one person's freedom, and Miz Violet stayed a slave so her child could be free.

Some time later, Miz Violet took Rosabel and hightailed it to California, found herself a likely wagon train, with folks who cared more about gold than freedom papers. Out in California, the buying and selling of human folks was purely against the law. Trouble was, they had this thing called a Fugitive Slave Act, meaning runaways who got caught would be shipped back to their owners. That's why the slave catcher came, and that's where the story of Freedom Hill truly begins.

The catcher was a regular bear of a man, with hard eyes and a disposition to match. He caught Miz Violet working in the boarding house kitchen, grabbed her in a tick, right in the midst of stirring up a mess of beans and greens and bacon for the boarders' supper.

When Rosabel saw the catcher take her mama,
she ran straightaway to Sophie's house. The family
was getting ready for their Sabbath supper when she
came knocking.

Soon as Rosabel told them what had happened,
they commenced to make a fuss over her. Mr. Kagan
said she should rest, and Mrs. Kagan said she should
eat, and all the Kagan children scurried to make a
place for her at the table.

Sophie gave her a handkerchief to wipe away her
tears. "We'll think of something, Rosabel," she said.
"Don't you worry."

Come sundown, Mrs. Kagan lit candles and said a prayer in a language Rosabel had never heard before. Sophie called it Hebrew. Then everybody wished everybody else a good Sabbath and got down to the business of eating. There was chicken soup with vegetables from Mrs. Kagan's garden, and a loaf of braided bread called challah.

The Kagans didn't exactly ask Rosabel to stay with them, they just acted like that was how things ought to be. Come bedtime, they put her in with Sophie. The two girls lay side by side, covers pulled up to their chins, talking a regular streak about how to save Miz Violet.

Best way they could figure to help Miz Violet was to buy her freedom, and that cost a plain fortune. Only way they knew to get that kind of money was digging for gold—so that's what they took a mind to do.

Folks surely did laugh when those little girls went into the hills with their pans and picks and shovels. They started out just watching prospectors at work. Next thing anybody knew they were washing rock and soil in their pans, swirling and twirling until everything was gone but the gold. In two days of trying, Rosabel and Sophie ripped their clothes, bruised their knees, and scraped their knuckles—all for less than half an ounce of gold.

"This will take forever," Sophie wailed, but they didn't have forever.

The slave catcher was moving through those hills, chasing after slaves the way other men chased after gold. He kept Miz Violet locked up in his old patrol wagon. Afore long, he nabbed a half-grown boy, then headed off chasing somebody else. Once that wagon got full, the catcher would haul everybody away. There'd be no knowing Miz Violet's whereabouts if that happened.

Mostly because nothing better came to mind, the girls went to see Mr. Thompkins at the assay office. He was the man who tested and weighed everybody's gold. Folks said he knew the hills better than any other living soul.

Mr. Thompkins had a fine idea. "You young 'uns oughta be looking in narrow gullies, piddlysquatting caves and such—places so small grown folks pass 'em by."

The girls thanked him kindly and went off to look for tight little places that grownups might have missed. They found plenty on that hill back of the assay office.

Sophie shinnied into a crevice so narrow she near got wedged halfway down.

Rosabel poked into a harmless looking cave and found herself staring into the bright glowing eyes of a fox. Rosabel screamed, the fox barked, and both of 'em tore out of that cave like a passle of wildcats was clawing at their heels.

Sophie fell down laughing.

"It's not funny!" Rosabel said, but next thing she knew, she was laughing to beat the band. When she was all laughed out, she crawled into the cave again.

"Sophie," Rosabel yelled, "I think I've found gold!
Come see."

Sophie scrambled into the cave. "Sure looks like
gold to me," she said.

It was gold, all right—a great, gleaming chunk of
it, and there was more, running all through a vein
of quartz rock. The girls dug up the nugget that very
afternoon and took it to the assay office.

Mr. Tompkins said the nugget was enough to buy Miz Violet's freedom, right by itself. "Now," he said, "let's file you a claim."

"What's a claim?" Rosabel asked.

"It's a piece of paper, says you two own yourselves a gold mine. That's the way of things hereabouts. You find it, you own it."

Rosabel and Sophie jumped up and down, hugging and squealing and laughing all at the same time.

By morning, the news was all over town. It spread so fast that the girls didn't have to go looking for the slave catcher. He came looking for them. Right in front of the assay office, he stopped the wagon and unlatched the door.

The prisoners stumbled out, all of them wearing shackles, all of them dazed by the sunlight. Miz Violet came first, with the half-grown boy behind her. Then came a lady with one blind eye, a man with whip scars all over his back, and a young woman near her birthing time.

Aside from being a mite thinner, Miz Violet looked none the worse for wear. Rosabel hugged her and Sophie hugged her, too. Then the three of them busted out crying.

The slave catcher unlocked Miz Violet's shackles and ordered the others to exercise themselves. They moved in a circle, round and round, leg irons clinking and clanking with every step.

The girls looked at those people and then they looked at each other. Neither one of 'em said a word. They just knew.

Rosabel took the paper out her pocket.

"Mister," she said, "we'll give you our claim to free the rest of these folks."

Well sir, people stood around thunderstruck, probably wondering if they'd heard right. That day, five slaves went free, a catcher went from hunting slaves to hunting gold, and a whole town learned a thing or two 'bout what matters in this old world of ours.

So, that's how Freedom Hill got its name. Leastwise,
that's the story. As for believing or not believing it, well,
reckon you got to decide that one for yourself.